A
Woman's
Need

by **Author Susan Collins**

DISCLAIMER

This is a work of fiction. Names, characters, businesses, places, events and incidents are either the products of the author's imagination or used in a fictitious manner. Any resemblance to actual persons, living or dead, or actual events is purely coincidental.

ACKNOWLEDGMENTS

Without you by my side none of this would be possible. You have given the me strength and courage to move forward in pursuing my dreams and for that I am eternally grateful.
I love you beloved.
-Susan

Table of Content

Acknowledgements

Chapter 1 "I Can't"

Chapter 2 "Impressions"

Chapter 3 "I See You"

Chapter 4 "Just Won't Stop"

Chapter 5 "The Cover Up"

Chapter 6 "It's Time"

Chapter 7 "Wrong Direction"

Chapter 8 "Spirals"

4

"I Can't"

Its 5:30 in the morning, the alarm clock is sounding, I roll myself out of the bed to take a shower and get ready for work. I must admit I don't feel like going to work this morning. My head feels like there is a construction worker drilling into the core of my brain. Can someone just come and kill me. Oh, the agony.

This pain that I feel right now comes from the drinking and club hopping I did last night. I can remember most of it, I think, until 10:00 o'clock, I think. I'm going to have to do a lot of thinking this morning because I just don't remember what else happened. What I did, or how I even got home for that matter. Let me give myself a little hand clap, clap, ouch this shit isn't funny, I don't think!

Can someone please remind me, not to mix my brown and clear liquors together again! Mixing those damn liquors have left me with a killer volcano erupting between my eyeballs. I need my shades, the lights in my bedroom hurt my eyes, my face, and my hair. Shit my teeth even hurt.

Oh, I'm sick, help, someone come help me, please. Temperare don't you hear me calling you?

Wait... who am I calling? Ugh, ugh!

There's no one here but me. Damn that's right. I'm alone. It's just me. I don't know whether to cry or laugh right now, but one things for certain, I still have a damn headache. Shit! Clap, clap, *Ouch stop clapping already that shit hurts!*

(As I'm looking for the Tylenol, I am thinking to myself) "Oh, if it wasn't for that Lyric and D'yVonne, I wouldn't be going through all of this hell right now"."

Drinking and divorce coupled with things on the brain just don't mix. But hey, what are friends for? Right uh huh, right! Just what are friends for (chuckling quietly to myself)?

We just had to go out. I couldn't say no! Now, my face is on fire and my eyes are erupting, while my stomach is waiting to spew hot lava chunks. I'm chuckling as I splash this cold water on my face, but shit ain't funny right now.

I cannot blame them, "What are friends for (this is too funny, but it's not really, this is painful, sad and hurts like hell)." *"Ouch!"* *"Ugh!"* I'm not clapping now that's for sure. Where's the toilet? Ugh!

Well, they tried to get me out of the house for some fun. Did I say fun already? Maybe it should be fun and relaxation. I hadn't been doing too much of the "fun" or "relaxing" thing since my separation from my husband, Temperare. They saw that I was struggling with being alone and still being in love with him.

Why does love hurt and separation feel like a pending execution sentence being handed down by a high court of the law of love and you're distended to be miserable?

Man, I cannot help but to think that this isn't real. It isn't happening to me and if it is just why? How could I have prevented it all?

I know full well that I did play a key part in the demise of our marriage and in the end of a friendship with Temperare.

That end was the end of it all.

But, I can't help to continue to think about him, his presence, his scent, his appearance, his walk, his smile, everything that made him--him. These are the things that I loved so much about him. Where did I go so wrong?

Did I start out wrong? I don't know. Yes I do, and I need to stop questioning it because I know all of the answers anyway. But I refuse to acknowledge any of the answers because every single one of them are all wrong. I would have to go back and question myself. Was I just a woman in need, I acted on my needs and desires and because of those factors now I have to think about this being a bonfire marriage, up in smoke? The marriage had lasted nine years. It was based on lies, deceit, fairy tales and mystical creatures all being a figment of my imagination.

I have a vivid imagination and told those lies so well, even good lies can be exposed, and everyone knows fairy tales don't exist. I don't even have to go into mystical creatures they came into play when my desperation was at a high point?

In the reality world, I'm waiting for the funeral director (divorce lawyer) to call and inform me when and where to show up to sign my divorce papers.

The final nail in the coffin that ends my life. Should I just put an end to it or myself?

Nah, I'm in mourning over a lost love not suicidal, at least not yet. But, oh, how I wish that there would be so much more that could have come from it instead of divorce.

I wish that I knew then, what I know now. But hindsight is a monkey of a different color, dangling in the tree of what would be called life. Sometimes, I feel like getting an ax and cutting down the tree of life, pouring out gas on that damn tree and setting it to a blaze, but I'm hurt and still in love.

I can recall the first-time that I met this man. He was walking down the hallway at the hospital looking like a smooth, overly stuffed, chocolate covered, mint green, Peppermint Pattie. He had shaved his head bald. He had this nice plump belly and wore green scrubs. Seeming him makes my mouth water.

I must tell you more about him, his name was Temperare. He was every bit of six feet tall and weighed about two hundred pounds. Dy'Vonne had the nerve to judge me! What can I say, I like mine round.

There was something about Temperare, his shoulders were broad, he looked like a logger that carried the logs on his shoulders. Those shoulders was long, broad and thick. Hell, he could have been a logger at one point and time in his life for all I know and his shoulders were the aftermath from the job. Just beautiful!

He had a chest like no one's business, it stood up high and gained attention when he walked into a room. His chest spoke for him, woman looked at it in amazement, those two bronze towers yassss. They held that scrub top in place nicely. Rock hard, yet, soft enough for me to lay my head on at night.

A few more things that set him off differently than most, he had this dick that would make a horse shy, a butt that I was jealous of and this little ass head. Sort of hard to believe that with all of that body and his tiny little head sits atop of it.

His skin flowed like a calm river from top to bottom. There were no scars. His lips were full and just right for kissing, and when he kissed me, it touched me to the deepest part of my soul. I have Temperare fever and no type of Acetaminophen can get rid of it. Yum!

With all of those flavors, nothing looked better too me. I wanted to taste every single bit of him, yup, luckily this isn't that kind of book, at least not yet, let me continue.
I had a sweet tooth, and he was my flavor of candy. Not only that, let's compound that with his handsomeness, intellect and pure genius.

I bet you're thinking that I must not get out much. Ha, well I do. See he was sixteen years older than I, yet, he acted as I did. Also considering, I'm only twenty-three that didn't matter at all to him either. Maybe it should have though, once again hindsight.

The older and wiser ones say that age doesn't make a difference, so that's how I looked at it. He was just an older man and I was what he wanted. And I thought that he had something that I wanted. Something that I needed and something that I longed and craved for. Maybe, it was just the fact that I was looking for the fatherly type of man that was stable in all of his ways. Nope, I don't think that's it.

Someone to show me unconditional love? No, I don't think so. I don't know. The fact was every time I saw this man my heart paused and mouth watered. I was lightheaded and I floated above the clouds. It was like I needed to breathe his air to survive. I was whipped!

Unfortunately, when I met him he was still involved with his children's mother, Kim (she's the tampon type).

That should have been the first red flag, but he said, "that they were having issues." The old issues excuses. I should have run for the hills and took cover under a bridge because usually when a man says those words "issues" he's a cheater.

But there was something different about him, I think! Maybe I was blinded by his intellect and I did what I normally do, I gave him the benefit of the doubt. Bad choice? Maybe not? Or was it?

I was a little skeptical at first, but he was so loving, kind and gentle, I needed that. Working five days a week, twelve days a week, a woman needs a loving touch at the end of the day. Even if the touch isn't her man's. That's what my brain kept telling me. Maybe I was setting myself up for destruction, but again, he was giving me what I thought I needed could I have asked for more?

"Impressions"

Each day of work started off the same it was like the first day of school, seeing Temperare walking down the hallway of the hospital. I didn't know sometimes whether to cry, laugh, or cry from laughter.

You just had to see that walk he had. It looked like a cowboy that had been on the horse way too long. You know one who has road rash. Whether he was trying to appear to be walking sexy or maybe it was his walk. I don't know, but wowzers. It was pretty sexy and even funnier all rolled into one.

But when he smiled my heart melted, no matter how I wanted to appear. If I was having a day from hell anything and all that should have mattered ceased. The noise stopped and phones were quiet. Doctors were silent and all I had seen was him.

When he made it too my space, the ten foot rule didn't apply, because my nose was euphorically delighted with the fragrance of his cologne.

He smelled of a European city, embraced in romance and caressed by flowers, but not an overbearing scent.

This scent left my mouth and nose tingling in a warm bliss from the aroma that it gave off. It was pleasantly delightful. Every time he wore this particular cologne, I would always have this fantasy of two people having passionate sex on satin sheets, in France or some exotic place, with the windows open and the women being pleasured beyond belief.

He was well put together despite his size and those green scrubs! Oh, I was just ready for him to say, "Hello".

Then he did just that. He said "hello and of course I replied, *"Hi Temperare and how are you today?"*

"You're smelling kind of sweet today, what cologne is that?"

My mouth watered waiting for him to answer. I was on his every word. When he replied, I was on it, *"Oh, this is some Naute, I bought at the mall the other day. Do you like it?"*

He could have been wearing cooking oil and I would have loved it. But I would not have told him that, so I calmly composed myself and replied, "Yes, you smell too sweet, Hun."

Then he come in closer, *"You smell beautiful too."* I chuckle. *"Seriously,"* he replied. *"I love that perfume on you, it turns me on every time I smell it, even before I see you. The scent, it hits my nose and the soft fragrance leaves a path and I know that you are in the building."*

If I didn't have a skeleton in my body, I would have been mush and a big pile of steaming wild rice, ready to be covered with his brown gravy. Keep talking though, I like it when he talks to me like that. (Then I softly lick my bottom lip and wink my eye at him so that he knows I'm digging his conversation)

Wait... I hear something! Someone's clearing their throat; it's not him or me. That tone sounds familiar, I know that this could only be one person.

That's right, I'm at work. It's that nagging ass Vida, this heifer could stop an orgasm in its tracks.
She's like a "*dam*" emitting electricity, and yet she was built in the middle of the desert where no water flows.

No people live and life ceases to exist there. I don't see how she was ever able to have a husband let alone any man. She always needs something.

I bet she drove that poor man crazy, come to think of it, I've never even seen him. He's probably a blow up and it's stuffed neatly in her closet until nighttime. Then she pulls him out and calls him daddy. Nah, even blowups need respect. Let me ignore her and then maybe she'll go away. Ugh, here she goes again!

Um, excuse me, you two," Vida says. *"You're excused."* Oh, did I say that aloud?

"Oh, Hi Vida, and how are you?"

(Thinking to myself, I would rather slap her in the face with my clipboard for disturbing my conversation with Temperare instead of saying hello, but let me play nicely).

"Well, I hate to break up you two, (yea right, I bet you hated to break us up), *but Mrs. White is on that buzzer again wanting her pain injection."*

You walked all the way down the hall to say that? Really?

"Vida, look above your name badge there's a little device that you can speak into and I will hear you." (You thirsty trick. I have an injection for Mrs. White alright, and you just want to talk to Temperare yourself, old lonely ass trifling triche. I thought to myself).

Instead of saying my thoughts I smiled and said, *"Oh, thank you Vida, let me go and see to her right now and get back to work".* *Temperare, I will chat with you later.* *"Okay Amillah, let's have lunch together, meet me in the cafeteria at 12:45 in our spot."*

Sure doll, I replied, as I walked away. I left puddles of hot steamy goo from our encounter, but this is not our first. These encounters happen every time Temp and I work near each other.

I think that our co-workers are beginning to notice my feelings for him. If they aren't wondering or thinking they should be. My hidden heart isn't so hidden anymore. Oh, but the feeling I have just being around him, his presence is soft and his touch is equally soft. My mouth waters, my fleshiest part of my womanhood needs his manhood to penetrate me. It's getting a little warm. I can't wait until lunch time so that I can bask in manly rays. Until, then let me get back to work.

Oh shit, Mrs. White and that damn pain shot, damn let me get over to her and give her this medication before she raises a stink about this damn injection. But, how can I work. Temperare is on my mind. Ugh, these buzzers are going off. I wish, I could clone myself so that my clone could come and do this while I just daydream about Temperare. Daydreams over, no clone and back to work I go.

Wait.... What time is it? Oh my it's lunch time.

"I See You"

I am so ready to see my Temperare. Did I just say that? My Temperare. Um, that sort of sounds nice, I like that. He's mine, but I don't think he knows it yet. He'll soon figure it out. Until then let me just keep reeling him in. Fish on!!

Oh, I have a minute or two, let me do my checklist, makeup (check), teeth (check), hair (check), clothes (dammit, I just have to be wearing these scrubs, well, let me push up these assets and rock these girls (check, check), okay, breath check (ugh, baby dragon breath, I got that quick fix. I have my trusty flask in my purse. One swish of some brown and he'll never know (check, check).

Just in time, here he comes. Oh that walk though. Now he's walking like he's on moving cotton candy clouds, yum. I can hear the soft violins playing, as he comes closer and closer to me. The music gets more intense, then reaches its climax once he's actually in my presence.

My heart is in my throat, yet, once again, I climax. I thought we were having lunch, first I need some water because my throat feels like I swallowed cotton. I didn't even realize that I was twirling my hair through my fingers. Damn, as I bite my bottom lip looking at this man.

He leans in to give me a kiss on the cheek, I instantly melt. I think, I melt daily and refreeze nightly.

"Hi babe, nice to see you again," he says.

Hi, you handsome. Then I chuckle like I'm a shy schoolgirl on my first date. Are you ready to eat? Um, yes doll, you can eat me all day, I reply.

"Wait, what's that smell?" Temperare replies.

"What's that smell, I ask?"

"Are they burning the bread in the cafeteria again?"

"That's probably what you smell I bet," I say.

Then, Temperare replies, *"Someone in here has been drinking because I swear to you I smell alcohol."*

Doesn't make sense we work at a hospital and some slime ball doesn't care enough not to drink on the job, yet alone at a hospital.

I swallowed deeply and try not to look guilty, and then say, *"Yeah, they're some people in here without morals."*

Then, I think to myself, Amillah, make sure you replace the brown liquor for some Vodka. It doesn't have a smell and still cures the dragon and then I chuckle.

"What's funny?" Temperare asks.

Nothing, just thought of a joke Dale was telling me at the nurse's station Temperareier (If he only knew, crisis avoided for now, check).

"Come on, sweet-thang, let's go and get some food into that fine round frame of yours," I say.

He agreed and grabs my hand and we walk into the food prep area.

"What are we eating today babe?" he asks.

I'm not sure, I want something light because I'm not feeling too good today. My stomach is achy and I feel the bubblies, I replied.

"A*millah!"* he replied.

"Yes, Temperare," I state.

"Um, have you had your monthly visitor yet?" Temperare asked.

"Monthly visitor? Oh, babe, please don't worry, we are fine. It's coming a little birdy told me. I'm fine," I said.

"I thought we were looking for food though, just to change the subject. Soup for me and what about you? I think I'm having a burger and fries, okay.

"Hi, Temperare...."

Hi, Temperare...... Umm.

"Hi," I replied for Temperare, as I turn around.

Here's that nosy bitch Vida again.

Where did she come from, I could have sworn that I left her at the nurses station caring for patients, I even left some of my patients for her to take care of just to make sure that she was extra consumed with her job. Man, let me give her a couple of death eye rolls, a lip smack and a hard head turn hair flip then maybe she'll get the picture.

Wait....It's not her lunch time, what the hell she doing here, she can spoil froze dehydrated veggies in a deep freezer, I thought to myself. But to save face, I asked, Vida would you like to come and eat with us?

"OH..." she replied.

Me, I'm not giving her enough time to finish her sentence. I came in for the kill; maybe she'll get the picture to back the fuck off.

"Oh, and okay, well you have a nice lunch then. I'll see you on the floor soon."

29

Now, finally, back to Temp. Temperare, I think we have enough time to eat and chat a little before it's time to head back to the floor, let's go before someone else comes and think they have a right to eat with us too.

Huh? Temperare replies. *"Why, do you say things like that Amillah? Do you want me all to yourself?"*

"Well.... yes I do, we work so far apart honey and sometimes I barely get the chance to see you. I just want the chance to be the apple of your eye even if it is only for an hour. Plus, I have to share you with doctors, trifling nurses and these nagging ass patients."

"Whoa, Amillah, we're here for the patients, it's both our jobs," Temperare replies.

"Are you okay, Amillah?" He asks.

"Don't mind me Temperare; I'm just in my feeling that's all. I know it's our job and I love my job," I reply.

Finally, we are at the table, my feet hurt (another measure to divert the conversation away from my previous overindulgence of feelings).

Mine is a little sore too, today. "*I think I will soak them when I get home,*" Temperare says.

"*Your home or mine,*" I reply?

"*Just come over to the house tonight and I'll give you a good massage. One you'll love and remember.*"

Then I smile.

"*Oh, I'll love huh,*" Temperare looks at me then winks.

"*Oh, yes, you'll love.*" I say.

"*Okay, what time?*" he says.

"Let's see, maybe around 9 o'clock or so. Does that work for you?"

"Anytime works for me when it comes to you," he replies. I chuckled.

"I bet you say that to all of the nurses on the floor huh?"

You're such a badass and I like that. I chuckled again to myself, because I was thinking about what he was saying to me.

"Well lunch time is over, are you ready to go back to the floor?"

"No," he replies.

Me either, I said to myself.

I'd rather just stay here and just look into your dreamy eyes and ram my tongue down your throat while we kiss. But instead of doing what my natural lust filled desires wanted me to do, I decided to head back upstairs with him.

So we walked to the elevator hand in hand like school age children. It felt so good, feeling his hand in mine. It was like holding onto cotton on a warm summer's day. Again, I could not hear anything, and see nothing. I was just in the moment with Temperare. I do not think that I could even hear him talking. That is if he was. I do think that he was enjoying the moment just as much as I was.

An unspoken moment of public display of affection without words, without extreme body language and completely beauty.

The elevator opens and we both enter. No one else is within sight and as the door to the elevator begins to close a hand comes into view, and then stops it from closing. Wait, that hand looks like, Vida!

This bitch! Man! I thought this woman cannot get a clue if you bought it and gave it to her. Better yet tattooed it on her body.

But Temperare being the man he is, "Oh Vida," let me get that for you and pushes the button to hold the door open.

Crap! Wet dream killer! *"OH thank you Temperare,"* she says.

"Vida, you're so welcome. Are you heading up to the floor with us or are you going?"

"Yes, I am heading up with you guys."

Then Vida smiles. I could have pulled all of her teeth out of her mouth with needle nose pliers and fed them to her. I need to figure out just how to get this chick out of my hair. She really thinks she's smart. I see what she's doing. She wants my Temperare. Guess what Vida, you can't have him (I think to myself). That smile you have on your face be careful before I permanently erase it, as well as your life.

I might just go and cut her brake line to her car.

Let's see how much she smiles as her car goes down one of those steeped hills she lives on. Yes, this is a good idea, but until I can get to you, let me go and handle Mrs. White before she gets on the buzzer again. It's time for her pain medicine.

"Temperare darling, it was such a pleasure eating lunch with you today. I will see you tonight."

"Okay Amillah," he replies.

"Vida, after you, let's make sure that our patients are a-o-k before our next break."

The elevator door opens and we all walk out with smiles.

I look over at Temperare and give him a wink, air kiss and we exit the elevator.

"Hey Vida wait up, why are you walking so fast? I thought that we were having a good time talking in the elevator?" I said.

Do you think, I was in the elevator for you Amillah, she says."

"Really, Vida, so now that Temperare is not around, you finally decide to show your true colors?"

"Why yes, Amillah," Vida exclaims.

"I could care less about you, all I want is Temperare. I see you two in the hallways talking and the smile that he puts onto your face, your glowing and the happiness. I want that!" Vida says.

"I knew it, but why pretend to like me Vida," I ask?

"Because I want to be in theater, why else would I pretend to like you? You do the same thing, Amillah, do you think that I don't know you hate my guts? Do you think that I don't know the looks that you give me are looks to disgust?"

"Well Amillah, lights, camera, action and watch me get your "man", I have a need and honey "your" dear Temperare will soon be "mine", but don't fret once I'm done you can have him back. That'll be my gift to you, my used rag. Oh and Amillah would you like to thank me now?"

"Why you little!"

"Shhh! Amillah."

We're at work, you wouldn't want everyone to know that we are in a not too friendly discussion about a man that is in a relationship would you, Vida happily shares?

"Oh, I see you Vida and now that you have shown your hand, I think that you just might want to watch yourself," I carefully declare to Vida not wanting to give my hand away too quickly.

"Things can get a little slippery when wet, you be careful, honey." I say to her because I don't want this two tone Slim Jim to know that she's just gotten under my skin and I could kill her now if we were not on this hospital floor with all of these people walking to and fro.

"Honey? Wait! Are you threatening me?" Vida says.

"Don't you wish, of course not? All I am saying to you Vida is watch for wetness," I reply.

"I do have to get to work, but you have a good reminder of your day."

(I smile on the inside, because now this chick doesn't know that she has just cemented her life on the asphalt road going to her home)

"I'm not done talking to you," Vida says.

"Yes, you are," I reply as I walk away.

"Just Won't Stop"

Just who does she thinks that she is? Oh, she wants my Temperare does she? I will give her something to want, something that she will never want to happen to her again.

What am I thinking, I can't do this -- this isn't right. Something's wrong with me. My mind is rushing with thoughts.

Just kill her and do away with her and that way she'll never be in your hair again. She'll never be in anyone's hair. Just because she wants your man.

But he's not my man he has a woman, we're just having a rough patch right now and he's looking for some friendship.

No he's looking for more than friendship, he wants to be your man and with her being in the picture it could ruin it all.

If he wasn't your man, he wouldn't be spending every waking moment with you, spending money on you, and trying to get into your panties every moment you let him.

It's more than about him getting into my panties, I love him, and he just can't see my true feeling for him yet.

Oh he sees your true feeling and he wants you. Don't deny him.

Kill her I say, I think it's the best option. The only option, that way you do not have to worry about her. Then you will send a message to everyone else that Temperare is your man and your man only.

But if I kill her I won't have Temperare. I will be in prison for life and then I won't get a chance to feel his touch on my skin, his lips against mine, the thrust of his penis inside of me, I won't have him. Then everyone else wins.

Do you want to miss it all just because you might go to prison? Do you want her to get it all?

So what if you go to prison, Temp will still come and see you. He might still come and see you. Maybe you two might even get married.

Get married, really? I don't think so, what am I thinking? What am I doing? There has to be a better way to get Temperare's attention.

Kill her I say! No! I won't do it! Leave me alone.

Wait! Nothing is wrong with me. Everything is wrong with her. Well if you won't do it, I will.

No don't do it, please, don't. I'm going back to work, I will not take part in this it's not right, I'm not going to jail or prison or even worse losing Temperare, because you want me to kill a person. That's wrong.

It's okay I will be here waiting and planning the perfect opportunity to strike on Vida, she'll never see it coming. I'm doing this for both of us.

I'm going back to work and I'm going to pretend that I did not hear any of this, matter of fact just leave me alone, do you hear me leave me alone.

I'm leaving this med room, do not say anything else do you hear me, I'm going back to work, the work that I love and will not lose because you won't me to do something foolish. Amillah tries to block these horrible thoughts out of her mind as she knows the difference between good and evil. She is struggling to tell her evil side No Way! Go away and leave her alone!

Now let's see, I have Mrs. White's medication, Mrs. Roberson's medication, Ms. Thompson's medication. Okay I think that I am going for these last rounds of the evening. I can't wait to get...

"Amillah!"

"Yes, Vida, what can I do for you this time?"

I don't even have to turn around because of that nagging ass voice, someone give me some damn bug spray.

I was under the impression after our last conversation that you finally understood that I wanted no dealings with you.

"Well, Amillah says, "Vida, *I do understand that, but I thought that I would just let you know that Temperare and I have a date tonight.*"

"A date huh? Sure you do.... Tell me what sleeping with his picture will do for you in the morning, okay."

"I've never seen someone so desperate in my life, there's thousands of men around here and you "just happen" to want this one. Are you just that thirsty? Does your vibrator need batteries? Wait, I know you're off your meds, that way you can have an orgasm, hahaha! Girl bye!"

"Oh, you think that you're so damn smart! Well, listen, you rail thin pale boney bitch, I've been so nice about this."

"This smile don't let it fool you, I'm all over your so called" "man."

"I think he likes the attention that I give him too."

"He likes all of this junk in my trunk versus feeling your bag of bones."

"He likes rubbing on these big perky titties, verses feeling on your dirt mound ant bites. When I let him come into this sweet black pussy oh, honey kiss his ass goodbye."

"Amillah, did you hear me, hello honey are you in there? Hello!"

"Why you low budget dirty movie, I say."

"Dirt movie! Girl yes"

"I plan on making one of those with Temperare. Would you like to see it when we are finished? I will send you a copy, what's your email? Hahaha!"

"See when my Temperare is around expect best behavior, but bitch this is me and you, no other nurses are around, no patients can hear us and no bosses walking the floor. Now what? Uh? Upset are you? Dizzy swirl!"

"Oh Vida you're full of jokes today aren't you."

(She didn't see, but I notice the director of nursing walking close up behind her) please tell me that joke again why don't you (then I smile)

"Pencil bitch what are you smiling at," Vida says rather loudly.

"Vida! What are you saying to your coworker says D.N. Winfrey. I need for you to go to my office right now, while I have a conversation with Amillah."

"Okay, Ms. Winfrey," Vida replies.

"Amillah, I need for you to be honest with me, *how long has Vida been speaking to you in this manner?*" Ms. Winfrey asks.

"Well, I cannot tell a lie."

(Knowing full well that I was going to throw Vida's fat sloppy ass under several buses and a plane)

"She has been speaking to me like this for some time now. I do not understand just what I've done to her for her not to like me, but I've tried everything. She's insulted me, my character, my performance on the job, tried to get patients to complain about my care for them, she even went so far as to botch my med cart."

"What! Oh, I cannot have that at this hospital. I will have a stern talking with her and rest assure when I am done she will have nothing but respect for you."

Ms. Winfrey replies with fury in her eyes.

"Oh, thank you I would really appreciate it." (For dramatic effect I shed a single tear)

"Oh and by the way Amillah, I do need to chat with you as well, but it will have to wait until tomorrow."

"Make it first thing in the morning after you clock in, what about Ms. Winfrey? Can you speak to me after Vida? That way I can get started to work when I arrive."

"Sure, but make sure that you are in my office in about an hour, okay. Okay. Let me pass these meds and I will be there waiting."

"Thank you Ms. Winfrey."

"Oh, you're welcome Amillah." Ms. Winfrey replies.

Let me scramble and get these meds done that way I can go to Ms. Winfrey's office.

I wonder what she wants to talk to me about. My mind is racing now. Geez, I'm damned if I do and I'm damn sure damned if I don't.

I need to get this job done because I need to help Vida fix her car real quick. Yeah, that's what I'm doing. She should not have pushed me.

I tried to warn her, but no she wanted to put her ambitions all into my face. Then she has the nerve to tell me about wanting my Temperare. Yeah this bitch has to go. Let me google, oh, this is it, got her.

Now, let's see how she handles that on her way home. She talked a big game, can see walk one (hahaha) check. I'll see you soon Vida!

Temperare tonight, yum (as I lick my lips) clap, clap, can't wait to see him. Let me go and clean up though, I don't want Ms. Winfrey to have any ideas just what I've been up to, and then I'll go and see her...

"The Cover Up"

How could I be in this situation, I thought I'd handled everything so carefully. After how I just helped Vida out, I'm sure she'll be out of my hair for a while, Google never lets me down.

Damn, let me speed up and get over to Ms. Winfrey's office. Now, here I am at the boss's office door, waiting on her to open it, hoping she'll say come in Amillah.

"Nice that you came," as she smiles.

Geez, let me compose myself. Remember to breathe before knocking, count to ten Amillah. It's okay, she just wants to tell you how wonderful of a job that you have been doing lately. Yeah, that's it! She's wants to tell me how good of a job I have been doing.

What am I worrying about, silly me I'm just fine, I've taken care of everything, okay let me knock on this door.

(I give the door a couple of soft taps, like a young child still scared because their parent called them into their room and you know that you've done something bad. Then, I followed up with a couple of harder knocks because I know she wants to tell me some good news and I can't wait to hear it.)The door opens slowly and there she is, the woman that runs it all, Ms. Winfrey, standing there like a C.O. Kill her with this smile.

"Well, hello again Amillah, I'm happy that you could make it here before you went home today. Please have a seat. I won't make this too long, so let's get straight to it. Okay."

"Sure, okay, anything you want Ms.Winfrey,"

(Let me throw her off her game real quick).

"I see that you have some new picture of your grandkids. Why yes, Amillah. I do. Most people don't even notice them. They are the joy of my life.

(I have a little surprise too; I just have to figure out my next move though, ugh! Let me move her along.)

"You do have a keen eye don't you, Amillah?"

"Yes, I do, there's nothing like family Ms. Winfrey. I can't wait until I start having children of my own."

(Now let me smile real big and continue to suck up because I think that she likes this) She just looks at me and smiles, I think I know what that means.

"Well Amillah, let's get to it. It has come to my attention that you and Temperare Prevost are having a relationship while at work and this relationship is distracting you from your duties while at work. Is this true Amillah?"

"Me and Temp, oh, no Ms. Winfrey, Temperare and I are friends and that's it. We have small talk just about every morning, eat lunch together from time to time, I've even babysat his children while he and his significant other had a date night."

(Wait, I think that's a little too thick of a lie).

"I complete all of my duties every day. I do not understand why someone would say this to you. I understand that employees must not fraternize while on the job, is in the rules and regulations. I love my job way too much Ms. Winfrey."

(Damn Vida I think to myself, but at the same time yeah you're big ass mouth just bought you a ticket that your ass can't cash, toodles Vida)

"Well, see Amillah, under normal circumstance there is an investigation into the claim of fraternization, but with you, I know that you do love your job and the patients here at the hospital. So just let this be our first little conversation and mind you if I have to have another little conversation with you the outcome will be very different because if there's one thing I hate it's a liar."

"I do understand Ms. Winfrey, I hate liars also and whoever is feeding these false statements about me please tell them to stop."

"It's ruining my good reputation and I've worked here for six year without any problems, so I don't want any now.

I love my job and the people that I work with and not to forget the main reason my patients, without them there would be no me."

(Got your ass, cheese)

"That's my girl, Amillah you are indeed a true peoples person and that's why I hired you."

"You are what this hospital needs. You have the brains, drive, determination and focus."

"Now, you keep up this good work and you just might make supervisor of the floor. I do have my eye on you for the position."

"Really Ms. Winfrey? Oh that would be terrific Ms. Winfrey, thank you."

"You'll know something by the end of the month, the key is keeping up to standards of excellence, but like I said I think you'll be a great fit for the floor. Thanks for stopping by Amillah. It's been a pleasure chatting with you."

"Rest assure that I will put an end to those nonsense rumors."

"Thank you again Ms. Winfrey and I won't let you down. Have a great evening."

(Damn I just coughed up a hairball, let me get my nerves together, I wasn't expecting that... Woohoo!)

I surely thought that she had my termination papers ready for me to sign at one point. I thought she was going to slap them on her desk, like she had a killer poker hand and she had just won the game.

But now I just won the super bowl of office visits and this feels g-o-o-d! I think Temperare and I need to have a serious conversation tonight definitely. I don't want the heat from our job working its way into our little thing.

Let me get home and get ready to see my cuddly, puddly, boogie bear.

Finally, someone I can hold onto and pretend like this day did not just happened to me.

Let me see the time. It's around 7:30, man those twelve hours are a killer on having a life.

But, that's okay, my baby will be here soon and I can't wait to hold him.

Let me get all bathed so that I will be soft, smelling good and looking like a warm, tall glass of milk ready for him to take a drink.

"It's Time"

Damn, I hear him knocking on the door. Okay, okay don't go running to the door looking all desperate and school girl crazy. Take your time and walk slowly and softly say *"I'm coming, hold on a moment please"*.

I can hear him saying, "Alright babe."

Ooh, I'm melting; let me grab a spoon because I'm not going to make it. I want to jump his bones as soon as I open the door. Okay, okay, pull it together girl, you got this. Now, do and handle your business. Open the door slowly and...

"Well hi stranger and then I smile, come on in. How's it going Temperare?"

"It's going baby doll, I couldn't wait to get over here to you tonight."

"Really, how so chocolate bear?"

"You know problems at home; again, I'm going to leave that chick I tell you."

"I see, thank you for reminding me that you do have a "girlfriend."

"I really needed that visual, buzz kill. I'm sorry coco bean, come over here and let me peel you and eat your sweet seeds."

"Oh Temperare, you're too funny."

Wait I thought that you had a date with Vida tonight.

"Date with Vida, are you kidding me?"

"She asked me to come by her house because her garbage disposal wasn't working."

"She wanted me to fix it for her. I told her that I would see what I could do, but I didn't make her any promises."

I knew that fat fuck was lying (I said to myself).

"Anyways, she called me just before I left and said she didn't need me to come, so I was okay."

"I'll see you at work tomorrow,"

"Then she said that she had the week off. Lucky her huh?"

"I guess Temperare, enough talk about Vida with her extra friendly do good self."

"Amillah come on now be nice."

"Okay honey, I will be nice, this time is for us and what we have planned.

"Boy do I have things planned for you tonight."

"Oh do you?"

"I do Mr. Prevost, but first things first."

I got called into Ms. Winfrey's office today and you'd never guess some little asshole has been spreading rumors about you and I having a relationship on the job. "I assured Ms. Winfrey that we didn't have anything going on. But, to just let you know because we both like need a job right?"

"Right!"

"Okay, so from now on we only fuck in the bathroom on the first floor, after noon, before two and in between three. Right?"

"Right! Wait!"

"What did you just say Amillah? You little devil you... Come over here and give me a kiss."

"Here I come Temperare, are you ready?"

"I've been ready and waiting for you all day long! Come over here to papa bear baby."

Instead of me wrapping my arms around Temperare, he wrapped his arms around me. He looked into my eyes as if he was looking into my soul. He then slowly and gently kissed me on the nape of my neck, while rolling his hand down the side of my breast as if he was patting me dry.

"Come baby, let's get more comfortable."

He then picks me up, while licking and sucking in between my fingers. He walked into the bedroom with me in his arm as if he was holding his most prized possession.

He laid me down onto the bed, took off his shirt button by button while looking at me with his big lips licking them, biting them, ready to come and eat the most interior parts of my pussy.

I wasn't ready yet for what he had in store for me. He grabs my hand and runs it down his chest and around his nipples. I then squeeze them and tease them between my teeth. Looking up to him as if I was waiting for his approval. He grabs my hair and pulls my head back to expose my full neck. He bends down and bites into me. Uh yes, I moan, oh that feel so good. He then runs his fingers down my lips as to say shhh, and as he continues to bite, lick and suck me, I moan louder, louder and harder, uh, uh, uh, yes babe I'm all yours.

Come closer to me, I say to him. I pull him even closer to me so that I can reach his nipples and then I begin to tease them again. Licking them swiftly like a kitten licking milk. I nibble on one and play with the other between my fingers, yes he says, harder, harder. I comply squeezing harder being rougher than I ever have before.

He then does the unthinkable, he moans and holds his head back with his eyes closed as if he's gotten the best erection known to man.

Neither of us was ready for penetration and this had to be the best foreplay that we had done in some time. But, before I knew it I was lying on my stomach, my shirt was off, and Temperare was kissing the center of my back inch by inch. His lips were so warm and his hands are so big, they held me tightly, *kiss, kiss, kiss, umm, yes, yes, yes*!

He then licks his tongue down under my panties and sucks one of my ass cheeks. Oh my gee..., he moves his other hand down slowly massaging my sides as he inches his way to my panties slowly, but surely he pulls my panties down and off.

Then, he reaches back up and grabs my cheeks with both hands, opens them wide and inserts his tongue into my ass. *Uh!* I sounded like a wolf baying at the moon because he had just hit my right spot. He goes in and out, running his tongue deeper and deeper into the tightest parts of my ass, licking the sides and grabbing my ass harder and harder.

Then, he bites me and I explode, my pussy is running like a river, my sweetest juices are escaping their confinement.

He lifts me up by my hips and bends me down deeper than before. I'm even wetter now and I can feel my sweetness drip onto the sheets. His fingers are caressing my clit, back and forth, with him still enjoying the pleasure of my ass. Then he inserts two of his fingers inside of me, with this rocking motion going deeper every time, I moan but not from pain it's pure pleasure. He's deep and I tell him to go deeper daddy, making me feel it.

"Yes, like that, now lick your tongue deeper into me and nibble, suck it papa. Yes, like that, don't stop.

Then he slowly begins to and rolls me over. I can hear his belt buckle clinking together as it and his pants fall to the floor. I look down and see his swollen manhood throbbing as if it had a heartbeat. He leans over; I open my legs wide because I wanted to feel all of him inside of me.

He comes in closer as if he was a panther on the prowl. I swallow deeply because I know that this love making was going to be one for the books.

No sooner than the thought came to my mind about our love making and how marvelous it was going to be, I was all ready for it, I needed this and I have been wanting this all week long.

This annoying buzzing, penetrates my thoughts, again and again.

"Stop, stop, and stop! What is that noise?"

"Don't pay it no mind Amillah, I'm ready for you."

"But, I can hear that annoying buzzing. What is that noise? Please don't tell me that's your cell phone! Really Temperare!"

"You couldn't cut off your cell? You might as well answer it because this mood has passed like a ship on ice!"

"Come on Amillah, come over here, I'm sure that I can make you feel it again."

"No, I think not (as I look at him with a side face and roll my eyes) *and there it goes again. Buzz, buzz, buzz, answer it dammit!"*

"Hello, yup, yup, I'll be there when I get there. What are you calling me for? You're worried about where I'm at? Really? Why? No need, I'm a grown man, I can take care of myself. Oh, really?"

(Now, I'm wondering what the hell he is talking about, because I already know whom he's talking too.

Oh, It sounds like she's mad, too bad for her, she should've thought about that when she was out smoking and choking with her next guy and I was entertaining her guy. I chuckle!)

You know what, I'll be home in a minute and we'll discuss that when I get there.

"Listen, Amillah, I have to go home and take care of something and I will be back okay?" (Huh he looks mad now, oh, so you have to go home do you, okay I'm thinking to myself)

"Be back Temperare? Huh? Really, now that's different, just like your phone being on is different. But, you go and do what it is that you need to do and I will be here when you get back." (He leans in to give me a kiss on the cheek. I reject it and look at him with anger. He swiftly gathers his clothes and puts them on and promptly leaves)

What the hell just happened! I needed him to caress my body, I needed him to make love to me with such vigor and passion, and I needed him! (I drop my head into the pillow and just breathe deeply as I lay there naked)

Thump, thump, thump.

Thump, thump, thump.

Let's me take you down.(music starts to play)

I only want to take you down.

Let me take you down.

I only want to take you down.

Let me take you down.

I only want to take you down. (I had fallen asleep and was awaken to my cell's ringtone)

"Hello, okay, here I come."

(Let me put on some clothes first because it's not that kind of party, I'm not going to the door naked. Plus, he left me hanging, so Temperare can stand outside for a few more minutes, I thought to myself).

"Here I come Temp," I say. I can hear him saying something, but I'm not too sure as to just what it is. I open the door and my mouth opened as well!*"What the hell is this?"*

"Wrong Direction"

"You love me right?" Temp asked me.

"Yes Temperare, I love you, but this is something that both of you should have discussed before you decided to dedicated me into your plan."

(Not only did Temp return back to my house, when I opened my door, I opened it to Temperare, his clothing in black garbage bags and Temperare was driving an old beat-up old LTD, just what the hell is a LTD anyway. This isn't the car we would go out in, I'm at a loss for words and I know my neighbors can see this shit).

"Come in, come in, hurry up, I don't want my neighbors seeing this. What, what, what are, what is, just what? I don't understand Temperare!"

"Amillah, I asked you if you loved me," Temperare replied.

"I do Temperare, but this I'm just, my mind, I wasn't expecting this. What about our jobs? This is a lot in one night. This isn't what our night was supposed to be like. Our night was supposed to be full of love making, passion, our desires being fulfilled and now I have to digest this. Just give me a moment Temperare, okay."

"I'm sorry baby, but I thought that you wanted us to be together Amillah? I thought that you couldn't live without me."

"I thought that I was your knight and you were my maid of honor, I thought that you were my queen, Amillah? What's really going on here? Were you only thinking of my dick as your knight, your king, your pole in which you would climb, what is it now that I need you?"

"You need me Temperare, because you got caught. Let's be frank about it, don't point nor ask too many questions unless you can Temperare handle the answers. Okay Temp?"

"Just what are you saying to me, Amillah? Give me a moment please; I don't want this to go into the wrong direction, so just give me a moment."

"Put your things in the spare bedroom; park your car in the garage okay. After that, I think I'll be ready for us to have a conversation about this right here, because we definitely need to talk about this right here. Okay?"

"Amillah, this is not what I wanted to happen. Just know that, I do love you and I mean that. Do you hear me Amillah, Amillah?"

"We'll talk when you get back into the house Temp, okay, I promise."

(All the while I was thinking to myself, Amillah you need a drink and you need one now, but you can't drink because there's a few things that you haven't been very honest with Temp about. Damn!)

Some time had passed and I'm sitting on the sofa listening as Temperare opens the garage doors then cranks this old car, pulls it into the space I had saved for my future luxury prized car that I was saving up for (damn what a waste) after that I hear the door lower.

I see Temperare walk in with an arm full of clothing and I say, "Is that it!" he replies, "Yes."

I know it's not a lot of stuff. Finally, I think I'm done. Let me put this away and I will be in here so that we can talk. A romantic evening ruined! Temperare comes in and sits next to me and holds my hand and opens his mouth to begin speaking, but before he begins to speak, I say to him, *"Let me tell you something."*

He replies, *"What is it?"* (With a look on his face as if he's shocked) and then I say, *"I'm pregnant!"*

"Oh, no! I asked you at work today and you said that the birdie, I just don't..." and Temperare drops his head and begins to weep.

I'm looking at the full magnitude of the situation in front of me and now I am without words. My emotions take a hold of me, then the tears flow like a mighty river breaking its measure of constraint.

Temperare then tries to console me, but we end up consoling each other, crying in each other's arms like we've just received news of pending death. This is not what neither of us wanted nor at this point needed in our lives. We realized at that point that we were consumed by lust and by us giving into our desires out of lust we had created an innocent life. What are we going to do?

(Drying the tears from my face)

"We really need to figure all of this out, I look to him for guidance in a matter of life altering change.

"I realize that Amillah. I'm so sorry this is my fault, I wished we'd used protection, I wished that we'd done something different," Temperare sadly states.

"I can't, not right now, handle this,"

Temperare drops his head *again* into his hands and weeps uncontrollably.

"Okay, okay, drying his eyes, I have it, he states. Let's just call into work and talk about this in the morning."

I agreed, then I got up to go to into the bedroom to make up an excuse, while thinking to myself this couldn't be just any old excuse. I had never called into work before, so I knew I had to make it good, and so I did.

I had a pending death in my family that required my attendance, so I would not be into work for a couple of days (I didn't realize just how true nor just how much time that I really would need off until later the next morning).

Later Temperare called the hospital giving his reasons for his absence.

After that we both pulled ourselves together, completely drying our eyes, cleaning up our faces, and then we walked hand in hand as if we were walking into a funeral, but in fact were walking upstairs to the bedroom.

Just a few hours before we had been in the midst of steamy love making. Now things had changed.

Little was said, maybe a glance of sounds that could have been words here and there, as we entered the bedroom. The smell of sex still lingered heavy within the room, as we walked into it. Sex was the last thing on either of our minds at that moment, because we had just entered into the danger zone.

The zone to which no "couple" should ever enter into, especially if they are not a "couple" by definition. We had not even gotten to the conversation about Temperare and his "baby mama" drama, because now I am his new "baby mama". Ugh! That just sounds awful, just me thinking it. Someone just kill me now, already please! I can't wait for the conversation in the morning.

I couldn't sleep, I tossed and turned for a majority of the night. I was also peeking over at Temperare to see if he was asleep from time to time.

I know that he was not, he couldn't be sleep after what I had just told him and then I heard it, the sniffle of sorrow and I felt awful again.

But why am I beating myself up so badly this motherfucker had something to do with this too. It's not like I was in this all alone right? Maybe, I should have just thought about myself instead of just giving into my desires. Shit!

I'm looking up at the ceiling wondering how I can fix this. Letting Temperare go isn't an option, but it should be an option because he isn't my man anyway.

An abortion definitely isn't going to happen. I would rather give the kid up for adoption or something.

Damn, I had to call into work, oh my, with my stellar attendance record and after the conversation with Ms. Winfrey did I just lose the promotion?

I think that I need to go back to sleep this is too much too soon.

I'm a mess right now and there's one thing for certain, I need to get myself together and get it together quickly before Temperare wakes up.

Where the hell is the sun at? I need for daylight to break through the fucking window, because I'm definitely ready for this conversation to happen!

Let me speed things up. *"Temp! Temp! Are you up? Babe? Babe can you hear me, wake up already, there's so many things that we need to talk about and you need to wake up. Please Temp, come on wake up!"*

"I'm up Amillah, I've been up for some time now," Temp replied.

"Thank God, I thought that I would have to figure all of this out by myself for a minute."

"No never, I'm here with you like I said *last night, or did you forget?"*

"No Temperare, I did not forget, but I was wondering there for a minute if you cared about our little growing situation."

"Don't remind me Amillah!"

"Wait what? Don't remind you? What the hell is that supposed to mean, don't remind you, I'm pregnant with your child and you're saying things like that to me! What is wrong with you? I thought that you said that you loved me! What is this?"

"Hold on hold on Amillah, stop for a minute and think okay! I didn't mean it in a negative way okay. I meant it in a positive way."

"How the hell is that positive Temp, don't remind you, sure Temp whatever you say!"

"I thought that we needed to talk about something Amillah, and already our conversation is going wrong. Where would you like to start the conversation?"

"Let's talk about why you are in my house with that old ass car in my parking spot that I have reserved for my future luxury car. Let's talk about this baby that we have made. Let's talk about our jobs that we could possibly lose due to the fact that we want to fuck at any given moment. Yeah, let's have a conversation, already."

"Well damn, Amillah really? I see that this baby has you bugging already, or were you just feeling a certain type of way because you saw the car that I was driving wasn't my normal car?"

"Well just for the record, I told my children's mother that she could have that one and I'd drive the old clanky one, I want my children to be safe while they're out and about with their mom."

"So tell me just what else is on your mind Amillah? What other problems or issues are "we" having that I need to know about that way I can address them one by one."

"Wait Temperare. I didn't want for this to start off on a bad note and it appears that -- that is what has happened. Can we start over? Please."

(Let me smile because I surely want to knock his head off right now I am beyond pissed at him. I think that I should be pissed at myself, damn!)

"Okay Amillah, I think that you're right, we are starting this off all wrong. I am so sorry for speaking to you like this. Can you forgive me? Just a little bit? Can I have a smile please?"

"Temperare, I don't feel like smiling. There's too much going on right now don't you get it."

"Yes, Amillah I get it," Temperare replied.

"So, why did you come back with all of your clothes?"

"Well, when I made it back to the house Kim met me at the door questioning me as to where was I at."

"I'm tired of lying to her, so I told her that I had fallen out of love with her and that I was tired of her bullshit. I was tired of her weed smoking and then I explained to her that the only thing that she did right was care for our kids."

93

"Then she was like she'd change. I would believe that Amillah, but she says it all of the time when she knows that I am at my wits end."

"I just want for her to get it together, if not for us, for the sake of our children, but that seems to be too damn hard."

"I made the decision to tell her that I had fallen in love with someone. Someone that is special, someone that doesn't do drugs, someone that cares for me and about me. That someone is you, Amillah."

"Oh, Temperare, babe I love you."

"Amillah, I need to finish telling you.

"Okay Temperare, go ahead."

"Well you see Amillah I've know that it's wrong to cheat on your woman, I get that, but I feel as if my woman cheated on me with all of her other extracurricular activities."

"I was the fall back and that hurt me Amillah. So when I met you and the attention you gave me renewed my faith in women, maybe I should have told Kim that I had fallen out of love with her a long time ago, maybe things would have been different but deep down inside I doubt it."

"I was Kim's caretaker, she knew that I would pay the bills, buy for the children and work my ass off to make sure that there was never a need. She took advantage of that and of me."

"But when I look at you Amillah, I don't see that. I see love, feel love and I like to taste your love."

"Temperare, hahaha" I say.

"No, for real though, Amillah, I love you! I know that it's a lot in one night, well less than twenty four hours, but I needed to tell you that. Understand?"

"I'm going to give Kim some time to cool off before I attempt to talk to her about our children and them coming to visit me over here. How do you feel about that?"

"We still have to discuss our baby Temp," I state.

"I am getting to that too Amillah, okay, promise," Temperare replies.

"See Amillah everything is so new. I've never left my children before, I usually stay and just endure it, but this time I felt that walking away from Kim was the best for me. Remember I'm walking away from Kim and never my children, I just want to make that clear to you okay Amillah."

"I understand that Temperare, but here's what I don't understand beloved. Why treat you so harshly if you're taking care of everything? Why did she not love you the way that you loved her? Do you still love her?"

"You've left me with more questions about your relationship with your children's mother than answers about what's next."

"I'm not sure how you will handle this answer, but remember that you asked the question Amillah, okay."

"I'm listening, Temperare!"

"Yes, Amillah, I still love Kim," Temperare replied.

If I wasn't so shocked already by his other woes of love that he was spilling about Kim, I would have drowned listening to this bullshit. If I didn't know any better I would think my house was just a crash pad and my love making keeps him from jerking off. Hm? Let me listen to this for a few more minutes before I interrupt again.

"Please continue Temp," I say.

"Well as I was saying, yes I do still love her, but that is because of the amount of time that we've been together. Amillah, you have to understand that. Love doesn't just go down the drain overnight."

It does if you remove the stopper, Temperare. I say to myself and then I chuckle.

"Temperare, get to our child and what are we going to do about him or her. Are you going to the doctors with me to check everything out?"

"Well Amillah, I feel as if you should terminate your pregnancy."

"Wait, what Temp! I know that you didn't just say that too me? I need to have an abortion? Really? Oh hell no!"

"Calm down and hear me out Amillah, please."

"You just told me that you loved me and then you said kill our baby in the next breathe."

"What human does that Temperare? Are you human?"

"Does my child's life not matter to you?"

"I'll tell you what Temp, let me handle what I need to handle and I'll get back to you when I get back to you."

"Can you understand that? I hope that you can hun-te-chile!"

"Come on Amillah. Let's talk about it like adults and just listen to what I need to say to you okay?"

"No, Temp, I'm afraid not. Since I have my own mind, and since my mind matters, I'm done talking to you now. I have appointments to make and other things to do other than talk to you about having abortions."

"We can discuss this a little later, okay!" Temperare replies.

"Only if you want to talk to yourself, I've stated my facts."

(Let me walk out of here before I end up in jail raising my baby).

"Spirals"

The conversation didn't go the way I wanted, I'm walking around now pregnant, I didn't want to tell Temperare, but I felt like last night was the best time to let him know that he indeed had another child.

I have to get it together, calm my damn nerves and clean up this damn house because Temperare's ass stank! I'm a girly girl and all of this manly shit in my house has to go or I'll sprinkle it with some nice perfume. Yeah, that's what I'll do.

Share my love? Well not love! That's what got me into this mess in the first place, but I can share with him this perfume. That way he can smell me wherever he goes. Good idea, Amillah!

Back to the happy things, let's see. I need to make some appointments to make sure a baby is safe in a two seater car, call the doctor, and make a note to self, because I don't want any stretch marks.

I like my two piece bathing suits way too much, I wonder! Can I still exercise the way I like? That is a very good question for the doctor. I want a woman doctor too. Just who would I like to deliver my baby? I would like to know if Temp is going to be in the delivery room. Oh baby, I'm happy that I finally told your daddy about you.

"Hey Temp, Temp, come here for a sec. will you please."

"Okay, here I come Amillah. What is it?"

"I was wondering if you are going with me to the doctors, so that we could see how our little bundle of joy is growing."

"Amillah, no! You can go, I told you have an abortion."

"Get out and I mean, my face and my house. How dare you Temp!"

"Fine, I'm out and I'll see you later."

"Oh, if I open the door Temp, you and your LTD can become lovers you fat flucker."

"Oh, that's how you're doing it Amillah!"

"Yes, that's how it is, and furthermore, until you can accept my baby steer clear for your own good Temp."

"Are you threatening me Amillah?"

"I'm sorry did that sound like a threat, Temp? I'm just stating that you should steer clear from me because I don't want your negative energy to upset my growing baby."

"One word Amillah, abortion, please do me a favor and just think about it, you haven't even tried to listen to what I needed to tell you."

"I'm not Temp and again, how dare you!"

"Temp, dismissed! Move along."

Note to self-stay away, far away from Temp for a while and decide if you're going to let him in the house.

Now, back to what makes me happy and that's my developing baby. Oh, I can't wait to tell my...... M'um? Who can I tell? None of those chicks at work? No one around here? Damn does my baby have to be a secret like my relationship with Temperare? That's okay baby, I'm still happy you're in there and soon the world will know about you whether your dad likes it or not.

I spent the rest of the day trying to enjoy my new motherhood and avoiding Temp like he was the plague. I couldn't even look at him now. The thought of him wanting me to abort this kid, oh that evil little father man. Just to think the night before he was my black stallion. Some stallion he turned into, more like an old ass mule. I should kill him and do myself a favor.

Night time came so quickly and morning even more rapidly. My morning routine was normal, but with a little twist, I actually was allowed to think about and say I'm pregnant.

Well as long as I wasn't at work. The drive to work was pleasant. Hell everything seemed the same, that is until I got off the elevator of my floor. My floor was eerily silent, no call lights, I didn't see any nurses milling around, for a minute I thought that I was on the wrong floor. To make sure, I looked at one of the room numbers and yup I'm on the right floor so what's going on.

I rounded the corner to the nurses station and all of the nurses were there, the doctors were there, Ms. Winfrey was even there, what the hell is going on I'm thinking to myself.

"Good morning everyone?"

I didn't even know should I say "good" or just "morning" and then Ms. Winfrey replied, "Amillah there has been a terrible accident."

I thought great Temp died on the way to work, now I don't have to deal with his ass, but instead I said, "An accident?"

Let me add some dramatic effect, so I place my hand over my mouth and opened my eyes real big. I did not even have a clue as to what was about to come out of her mouth next. I don't think that I even cared.

Then she said, "Vida was in a horrible car accident the day before."

Oh shit, I forgot all about that clown and her clown car that I fixed for her. Okay Amillah, show no signs of happiness, I said to myself.

"Vida was in an accident?" Oh no, no! Let me shed a tear or two.

Then I said, "Is she going to be okay?"

However no one answered.

"Okay why are you guys' so quiet?" Again I asked, "Is she going to be okay."

Then everyone began to look at each other, but Ms. Winfrey answered, *"We don't know Amillah."*

I can hear police walkie talkies in the background, damn the cops are here, now everyone is looking at me.

I'm just being paranoid, I'm fine, until I felt a finger poke my shoulder. Oh shit it just got real.